In every generation,
there is a chosen one.
She alone will stand
against the vampires,
the demons, and the
forces of darkness.
She is the SLAYER.

Buffy
Summers
7th period

Little, Brown and Company
Hachette Book Group
1290 Avenue of the Americas, New York, NY 10104
Visit us at LBYR.com

First Edition: September 2018

Little, Brown and Company is a division of Hachette Book Group, Inc. The Little, Brown name and logo are trademarks of Hachette Book Group, Inc.

The publisher is not responsible for websites (or their content) that are not owned by the publisher.

Library of Congress Control Number 2017961043

ISBNs: 978-0-316-48023-9 (paper over board), 978-0-316-48022-2 (ebook), 978-0-316-48026-0 (ebook), 978-0-316-48024-6 (ebook)

PRINTED IN THE UNITED STATES OF AMERICA

LSC-C

10 9 8 7 6 5 4 3 2 1

Buffy
the vampire slayer

NEW SCHOOL NIGHTMARE

Carolyn Nowak

LITTLE, BROWN AND COMPANY
New York Boston

Dear Diary,

Mom thinks writing in you will keep me from getting into trouble. She thinks I need to express myself! She thinks I need to reflect on my feelings! I told her that I wouldn't have any big, dumb feelings to reflect on if she hadn't taken me out of my old school and moved me to the worst, boring-est place anybody could ever imagine: CLEVELAND!

Lake Eerie

Diary, I can't understand **why she'd do this to me!** I'm starting middle school soon—like, tomorrow soon—

Cleveland

OHIO

and I won't know a single person when I get there. Maybe I'll try out to be a cheerleader.

I can jump higher than any other kid I've ever met so I think I have a chance.

Anyway, you dumb empty book, I'm going to stop writing in you and go to sleep instead. I hope I dream of...

California sun

or lemon trees

or the beach.

But I know when I shut my eyes I'll see the same thing as always: **vampires conquering the world.** Why do I always dream about vampires? They're so icky and gross and bitey! Blech!

Buffy

Yay. First day of school. This is my new class schedule:

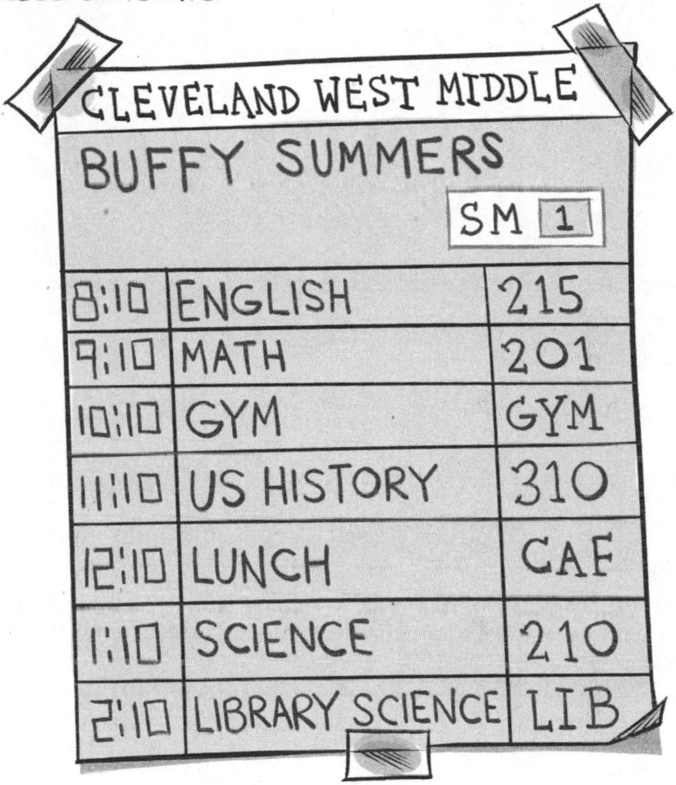

CLEVELAND WEST MIDDLE

BUFFY SUMMERS

SM 1

8:10	ENGLISH	215
9:10	MATH	201
10:10	GYM	GYM
11:10	US HISTORY	310
12:10	LUNCH	CAF
1:10	SCIENCE	210
2:10	LIBRARY SCIENCE	LIB

I can't believe gym is still required. I'm practically an adult now. I've got more important things to do than run in circles.

And why have I been signed up for TWO science classes? Am I being PUNISHED?

Hey Diary, what's new?

Just kidding, you're a book.

Well, my first day of middle school was about as dumb and boring as I thought it would be. I think my bike got all shaken to bits in the cross-country move. I don't know how I survived the flight over my handlebars, but I almost wish I hadn't cuz I ran smack into this girl with really good hair, and everyone who saw had a real good laugh at my expense. I don't think "Blondie" is technically an insult, but she sure made it sound like one.

Class is boring, and I have nobody to talk to. Oh, except for library science. I still don't know what the class is supposed to be about, but the teacher (Miss Sparks) is a real wacko. Who hired this lady? She talks like a wizard, goin' on about all kinds of crazy stuff like (get this...) VAMPIRES! And not just that, but, like, the phases of the moon, and the color of

monster blood, and shoe sizes for killer clowns
and the difference between Bohg'Dar and
Brachen demons and what kind of wood makes
the "best steak." What do steaks have to do
with vampires?! She told me that I'm the
"chosen one." And she was all, "This is the
thrill of living on a Heckmouth—one has a
veritable cornucopia of fiends, devils, and ghouls
to engage." And I was all, "I think I speak for
everyone here when I say, 'HUH?'" She might be
a crazy person. I think by "chosen one" she just
means "the only kid unlucky enough to get stuck
in this class."

   I hope I can switch out. I can't associate
with this lady! I'm new at this school and I
don't need that kind of reputation!

   I mean, vampires? Yeah,
right! Vampires aren't real....
   Are they?

Dear Diary,

The Earth is huge. I mean, I think it is. I haven't seen very much of it. But I'm telling you, there must be some place on this big, big planet where a girl can just go and be herself. Someplace where she can walk around without feeling like the biggest friendless loser. I want to find a log cabin to live in and never, ever go to school again. I keep making a total fool of myself. And, like, destroying property. One kid called me Destructo Girl. And I was like, "Yup, Destructo Girl, that's me."

I'm still mad at Mom for moving me out here. But she promised to take me to a movie tonight because she says she knows I'm trying to make the best of it. I really am! Like, I still go to library science, where the teacher keeps saying she's my "Watcher." Crazy! Watching me? Why? Miss Sparks is even weirder than I thought. Not only does she talk about vampires, like, <u>ALL the time</u>, but she wears the same thing every day except for her tie, which is always different. Here are the ties she wore this week:

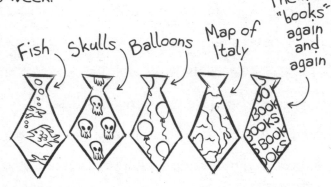

Fish   Skulls   Balloons   Map of Italy   The word "books" again and again

I mean, she irons her jeans! She's evil! I tried to tell Mom, and she said "Respect your teachers, young lady!" Oh well.

Anyway, Mom's hollering for me! Movie time!

Dear Diary,

I have to write this all down right now before I start to confuse it for one of my dreams. I think I killed a <u>REAL</u> vampire. Me. Kill. Vampire. Vampire?? I think that's what she was? Her face got all weird and she had <u>fangs!</u>

BEFORE   AFTER

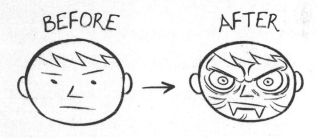

Just a guess. My heart is still beating so fast! I was so terrified when she grabbed me, but then I felt power surge through me and I just kicked! I kicked her right up into the air, even though she was huge! I must have kicked her pretty hard, cuz she flew backward and (kinda sorta) got impaled by a tree branch. Now this is the weirdest part: She turned into a bunch of bats, and they flew away. I didn't know what to do, so I just went back inside the movie theater and pretended everything was normal! (I mean, sure, yeah, I was shaking, but I didn't want to freak out my mom.) Mom asked me if I wanted popcorn, and I almost said, "Did you know that vampires are REAL and that I just killed one?" But I couldn't say that so I just said, "No," which was pretty stupid because I love popcorn.

The whole night has me freaked!! I need answers!! Unfortunately, I think I know exactly where I can get them—from kooky Miss Sparks. (Maybe she's not so crazy after all.) Guess I'm actually looking forward to going to 7th period on Monday.

The movie wasn't even that good!

How to Kill Vampires:

Where vampires might hang out:

- cemeteries
- basements
- nightclubs
- 24-hour diners (only at night)

Vampire weaknesses:

- stake to the heart!
- holy water
- garlic
- crosses
- the sun

I love to kill vamps!

Dear Diary,

Okay, it turns out Sparky is kinda cool. (Sparky is what I call Miss Sparks now. She tells me not to, but I think she secretly likes it.) Anyways, like I was saying, Sparky isn't so bad! She's still a goof, don't get me wrong, and I'll never understand her choice in ties, but she does know just about everything there is to know about monsters and vampires. And even though she's a big nerd, she's teaching me how to fight! At first, I thought fighting vamps was gonna be all stakes and holy water, but apparently there's a lot of kicking and punching involved, too. Vampires are natural fighters. That's why I have to train every day. It's a lot of work, but I'm kinda having a good time.

Every day, for my last class, I report to the library. Sparky and I push aside all the tables and chairs, then she puts on all sorts of funny pads to protect herself—against little me!

Why? Because it turns out, being the "chosen one," or "the Slayer," means that I am SUPER strong. The other day Sparky jumped at me, and I tossed her right over my head like she weighed nothing. Buffy-1. Sparky-0.

Come at me!

Oh, I almost forgot the best part! Sparky made a vampire sock puppet. I named him Carl. He's supposed to be

intimidating, but he's <u>soooo</u> gosh darn cute. I don't even wanna hit him. But I gotta punch anything with fangs. Slayer rules. Sacred duty, yadda, yadda, yadda.

Tonight, Mom made spaghetti and garlic bread. Garlic is, like, total poison to vampires. No wonder I love garlic bread so much! Mom told me it seemed like I was in a good mood. I am. <u>Being a Slayer is cool.</u> Time for bed!

Dear Diary,

It's amazing that I can still hold a pen. I'm so tired!! Between being a Slayer and a student, I never have time to just relax. It's like I have two jobs: being normal-student Buffy Summers, and also being Cleveland's personal vampire Slayer. I only get to sleep, like, four hours a night. Ugh! I feel like a zombie! Actually, Sparky would want me to clarify that zombies <u>can't</u> be tired—they're dead. (By the way, did you know zombies are <u>REAL</u>?! At least, that's what Sparky said. Yikes.)

Zombie

Braaaaains.

ZomBuffy

Sleeeeep.

Both have
• dark eyes
• drool
• dirty clothes

* Buffy <u>does</u> have better hair.

So, yeah, I'm <u>dead tired</u>. The other day, my training sock puppet, Carl, even got a lick in, smashing my face and giving me a bloody nose! Sparky felt so bad that she brought me a soda from the teacher's lounge and let me drink it right in the library. Usually she's all, "No food or drinks near the wonderful, precious books!" But she made an exception. Oh, and get this! My nose stopped bleeding almost right away. Cuz I'm the Slayer, Sparky says I heal quicker than most people. Rad, right? But how come I have superstrength and super healing but not super-stay-awake-in-class powers? I fell asleep in class again today, and my teacher was all:

Even Mom has noticed. She keeps asking why I'm so tired and if I'm okay. I wish I could tell her, cuz I hate lying to her. She's a pretty cool mom, all things considered, but she'd freak if she knew about my little study-and-fight-club with Sparky. Sometimes I pretend Buffy and the Slayer are two different people (like twins). Buffy goes to school and does normal stuff like homework and movie nights with Mom. The Slayer is vampire-hunter girl who has to punch a librarian and her sock puppet every day. I guess being two people is neat—just exhausting. The sad part, though? Neither of us seems to be very good at making friends. I miss having friends. But since I'm the Slayer, would I have to lie to them, too?

I guess you're my only friend, Diary! Just kidding, you're a book. I'm not crazy. Yet.

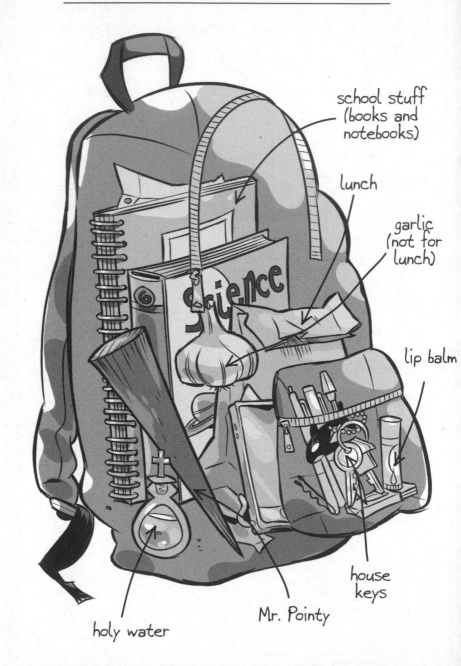

Dear Diary,

Last night, I had my first OFFICIAL vampire-battle! Swoosh! Stab! Poof!

Sparky was so proud when I told her about it. That silly old vamp really thought he had me, too. Not today, Cowboy! Unfortunately, I ruined my new jeans fighting a second vampire. Mom was furious when she saw them. If only I could tell her it was all to avoid getting eaten by a vampire and make Cleveland a little bit safer. Instead, I told her I took a shortcut and fell down, which is kinda true! Anyways, she gave me "angry-Mom" face and told me to stick to the sidewalks. Sigh. I really liked those jeans, too.

On the bright side, all my training with Sparky is finally paying off! I think it's really lucky that I was the one who got attacked by the vamps and not someone else who couldn't handle them. But it makes me think...How many of these batty baddies are hanging around this town? Am I going to have to *poof* them all? Am I even up for that? Seems like I'm only gonna get busier from here on out, which probably means I'll never get the chance to try out for cheerleading.

Do you hear that, Diary? My pillow is whispering, "Buffyyy, Buffyyy, come put your face on me." I better do what it says....

Off to Dreamland,
Sleepy Buffy

Dear Diary,

I don't want to make you jealous, but I made some <u>friends!!</u> Their names are Sarafina and Alvaro, and they invited me to go trick-or-treating with them! Mean Girl Melanie said that trick-or-treating is for babies, but Sarafina told her, "Go ahead and talk yourself out of free candy all you want. It just means more fun for the rest of us." "That made me really happy, because <u>I LOVE HALLOWEEN!!</u>

And I really love my new friends. It's a relief to finally have people to talk to at school. Even if I can't tell them everything.

Sparky says not telling them about Slayer stuff is for their protection, and I get it. I just hate lying to everyone. Friends aren't

You must keep your social life and your Slayer duties separate. Being a Slayer is a secret!

supposed to lie. Of course, most friends aren't vampire Slayers....

I'm tired from school and Slayer duties, but I am so excited about Halloween. All that sugar and candy. <u>Mmmm.</u> There is no problem that cannot be solved by chocolate. Now I just need to figure out what I should dress up as....

IDEAS FOR HALLOWEEN COSTUMES!

Princess
(No—
vampires
could ruin
my dress)

Wrestler
(No—
spandex is
weird)

Mermaid
(I couldn't walk, let
alone kick!)

Red Riding Hood

Stake
in basket.
Perfect!

*Note to self:
Don't forget to bring Mr. Pointy!

CLEVELAND PUBLIC SAFETY

STAY SAFE ON HALLOWEEN
- •DON'T talk to strangers!
- •DON'T stay out after dark!!
- •Best not to leave the house at all!!!

Hah! Check out this flyer Sparky made. She's been handing it to all the kids at school. Her heart's in the right place, but does she really think kids are going to stay home on the best night of the year? I know vampires are real and I'm STILL going out!

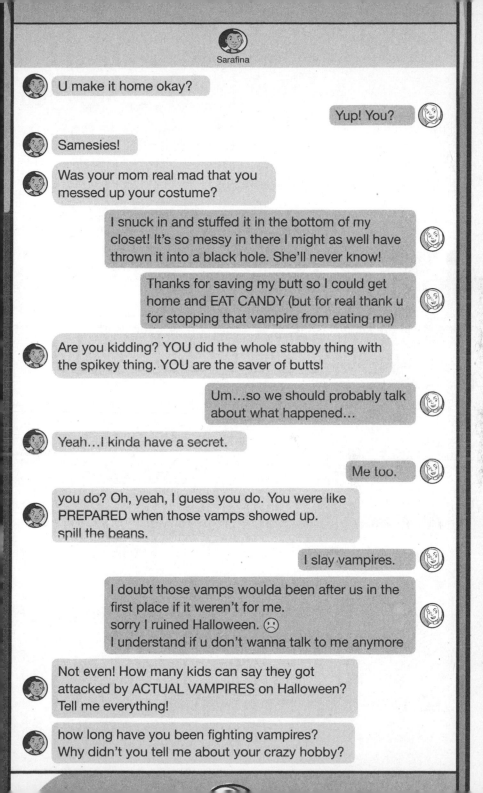

Since I moved here.
it's supposed to be a secret!

sorry, Sparky gave me strict
orders: TELL NO ONE!

 Sparky? You mean Miss Sparks,
the wacko librarian?

Yeah. She's introduced me to my *~destiny~*
as a vampire Slayer. She's been training me.

NO WAY! I KNEW there was something
weird going on with herb.

her
But I thought maybe she played bagpipes or was
into extreme knitting or collected porcelain turtles or
something. I never imagined she'd be a cool
vampire-fighting coach. Wait--can she train me too?

Waitaminute!
you still haven't told me how you
made Mr. Pointy go all floaty

Mr. Pointy?

I named my stake. Don't change the subject.
your beans. Spill em

So I'm a witch.

That is so…

Weird? Freaky? Psycho?

AWESOME!!

You really think so?

Totes

Think Miss Sparks would train me too?

I don't know. Why don't you drop
by 7th period? We can ask!

Cleveland Times

BLOOD BANK ROBBED AGAIN!

"It's my solemn pledge to the residents of Cleveland: I will put a stop to these rather ridiculous robberies," said Chief of Police Roger McKay. "What these creeps are using all this blood for is not my concern. But I'm sure it's something really, really gross."

Local Birdwatchers Report Disturbing Rise in Vampire Bat Population

"They aren't birds," said local avian enthusiast Susan Brown. "I have to stop myself from recording them in my logbook every time I see one. It's very frustrating."

Strange Men in Strange Costumes Cause Commotion in Coventry Village

Local 911 operators were overwhelmed on Sunday night with a flood of reports describing "spooky teens" in "Victorian garb" who were "acting generally mischievous." Though some residents of this eclectic Cleveland village claimed a jovial "kids these days" defense of the youngsters, others seemed to find the activity somewhat more sinister.

Buffy's Stuff

Library Science

Message

Vampires everywhere! - Inbox

TO: Buffy Summers
FROM: Miss Sparks
SUBJECT: Vampires everywhere!

Buffy, have you seen the news? We must talk!

Sparky

 Buffy,
It pains me to resort to this crude form of communication, but I thought it might be the best way to reach you on short notice. You have not responded to my email. The local vampire activity seems to be increasing at an accelerated rate in recent months, and I think it would be wise of us to react in kind.
Sincerely, your Watcher, Miss Sparks

OMG! YOU ARE HILARIOUS, SPARKY!

It's text messages. Not letters from WW2. You don't have to put your name.

 Buffy, this is very serious. We need to respond quickly.

You mean more stabbing and stabbing faster? 🔪🔪🔪😬

Yes. I suppose so. I would like to patrol tonight. Please meet me at 10 PM.

☹️ Ugh! I have homework! Also, I have a curfew!

You have a sacred duty to protect the world!

Double UGH! Fine! but if I get caught sneaking out, YOU are telling my mom the truth. Also you have to bring me a soda! Sugar! Caffeine! It's my Slaying fuel! I need it! For my destiny!

 I'm not sure "drinking soda" is an essential part of being the Slayer, but I'm too busy to look it up.

🗑️ see you later!

Dear Diary,

Things have been <u>rough</u> lately. That's why you've seen a lot less of me. I don't have time to blah-blah-blah all over your pages so much anymore because my Slayer duties have gotten a <u>lot</u> more intense. Sparky's making me do all kinds of nighttime patrolling.

Last night, I fought my oldest vampire ever. Sparky didn't think it was funny, but I could hardly stop laughing cuz he looked like a cartoon of <u>Leonardo da Vinci.</u> You'd think a vamp that old woulda learned to be less obvious and dress modern. Instead he was wandering around the woods, big old beard and funny hat and long dress, thinking he looked real scary. Sparky is all business usually, but I'm pretty sure she cracked a smile when I did an impersonation of Leo da Vampire. Anyways, I got

Where art thou?

home just as the sun came up. And it's not the first time I had to stay out so late! Apparently Slayers barely sleep. Not cool. Sparky says I can handle it—or rather, my body can—because it's the body of the SLAYER. I can feel the extra strength all over. I can jump higher and punch harder every single time I fight. But I don't care. I miss sleep!

Does that sound dumb? Cuz it's so not. I miss pillows and sheets! I miss lying in my bed, lights off, and stumbling into dreams. Or even lying in bed awake, thinking about TV and clothes and kittens. I think I just miss the space in my brain that I used to use for thinking about that kind of silly stuff. Now my fun brain is all dusty. It got replaced by dusty, old vampire folklore. (And techniques for doing the best high kicks.)

Dear Diary,

Look! Another FUN note that Mom left for me...

> Buffy,
> I have to work late, but when I come home, I expect to see your room clean and all the dishes done! I can't be the only one who cleans around here, young lady!
>   Love, Mom

If only I could say, "Sorry, Mom, I can't do my chores, because I'm sorta busy saving the whole city from vampires! Oh, _and_ going to school, _and_ doing homework, and SOMETIMES (if I have, like, ten seconds to myself) doodling in my diary and feeling like a normal girl."

Sigh. Time to wash plates. Hope I don't fall asleep and drown in the sink. Sparky would be pretty disappointed if dirty dishes were the thing that did me in.

-Buffy the dish-buffer

Sleepy Buffy

Drool

To-Do:
- Louisiana Purchase worksheet
- Sharpen Mr. Pointy
- Go with Alvaro to pick up film for his camera
- Give Mom shirt with mustard stain to send to dry cleaner

~~History Notes~~
Slayer Stuff

VAMPIRES

- Super strong
- Heal fast
- Night vision
- Immortal! (except when they meet Mr. Pointy)
- Good sense of smell (like dogs!)
- Drink blood (super gross)
- They don't breathe. (weird!)
- They don't have reflections. (creepy)
- They can't come into your house unless INVITED.

Hello!

THE SLAYER

- Human girl chosen by fate
- Super strong!
- Super fast!
- Super durable!
- Super cute! (citation needed)
- Vampires are terrified of her!!!

THE WATCHER

- Member of the Watchers' Council
- Devoted to tracking the activities of demonic forces on Earth
- Trains and guides Slayers
- Should always buy milk shakes for Slayers as a reward for a job well done!

Sarafina

 Hey Buff! What's doing this weekend? Wanna hang?

Fina!

I miss hanging with you. sorry, I've been staking vamps left and right and up and down.

Did I mention I miss hanging with you? 😢

 Same here!

Any chance you can hang out tonight? I'd be down to do more training 💪

Or you could come to my house for TV-watching
and my mom's signature triple-baked ziti. (It's DISGUSTING and I could really use your help eating it)

I can't 🙁

I have to go on graveyard patrol with Sparky.
Lots more vamps to take care of. Gotta keep Cleveland safe.

 Graveyard patrol? Sounds cool! Let me come!

Sparky wouldn't like that.

 Who cares?!

Good point! Meet me in the front hallway after school!

Dear Diary,

I have to tell you about this <u>amazing,</u> <u>amazing night</u> I had! First of all, I think I finally understand long division. And who explained it to me? My super-smart best friend, SARAFINA! She came along on patrol with me and Sparky, and she totally saved the day with her crazy-incredible witch powers. She says she only knows a handful of spells and that a bunch of them are useless (like a spell that removes static cling from clothes), but tonight her rando magic totally came through and helped me stake a vamp. Then Sparky bought us milk shakes. (We convinced her we deserved a reward. Well, Sarafina did. Sarafina is super persuasive. It's not witchcraft—just good grades in debate class.)

While Sparky drove us home, Sarafina told us all about how her grandma taught her and her sister magic so they could use it to help out with chores and stuff. Sparky thought maybe the magic was a thing that ran in Fina's family, but Fina says her grandma actually learned it from a green-haired girl working at a dentist's office, and the green-haired girl learned it from the internet.

But to be a witch, you gotta have a special mind and spirit to really make it work, Fina says, like her and her sister and her grandma, who are really in tune that way. Their powers get stronger when they're all together. Cool, huh? I'm excited to learn more about magic, but I don't think I can cast spells myself. That's fine, though. I'm still the best at PUNCHING!

Usually I'm just tired and dirty after vamp slaying, so this was the first time I was sad about patrol ending. Now I can't wait to go out on another one so Sarafina and I can work together again. We're a great team. I think she's amazing.

Gotta crash now. I am very happy and very full of milk shake.

SHAKE HUT

Dear Diary,

Is it weird that I'm more scared of Melanie
than I am of vampires? That girl is **mean**. And
I mean terrifying. Ugh. Whatever. I have bigger
stuff to deal with....

Thanksgiving is tomorrow. It used to be my
most fave holiday, what with all the stuffing
and pie and watching the parade on the couch
with Dad....Now Turkey Day makes me all sad-face.
Holidays aren't the same since Mom and Dad
got the big D-word. (You know, d-i-v-o-r-c-e.)

Last year in California, Mom and Dad were
still together, and we had dinner on our back
porch. (Definitely can't do that here in Cold
City! Brrrr!) Anyways, Dad forgot to put sugar
in the cranberries, so they tasted like sour
death. Even though Dad really screwed up the
cranberries last year, I wish he was here to
screw up some more stuff. I don't know....It's
frustrating to think of having dinner without
him. Every year he asked me to make hand

turkeys to use as decorations, and I always hated it, but now I <u>wish</u> Mom would tell me to make a few stupid paper gobblers to go around the house.

I kind of want to chill out and be sad about missing my old life, and I kind of want to get really angry and stick some vamps with the pointy end of a stake. Which I really could do, cuz Sparky has been bugging me about keeping up my slaying duties over the

Vampire Slayers have been working on Thanksgiving weekend since before Thanksgiving even existed!

holiday weekend.

But I'm all slay, all the time, so I told Sparky, <u>NO WAY</u>. I'm taking a vacation. Sure, things are getting pretty spooky out there. But if I'm feeling bad about this year's Thanksgiving, I bet Mom feels even worse. I want to stay by her side as much as I can. Sparky can go it alone if she has to.

Better sleep! Got lots o' food to eat tomorrow!! I'm a growing girl!

Dear Diary,

Okay, okay. This was actually a <u>great</u> Thanksgiving. Sparky showed up just in time for dinner because she was gettin' chased down by two super-old Swedish vamps named Hugo and Agnes. A couple of serious baddies, but not too smart. One of Sparky's friends in Europe apparently heard a rumor that they were shipping themselves over in a couple of barrels—they were just real determined to get to Cleveland for some reason. I guess they wanted to meet me so I could totally kick their butts.

I stuffed my face while Mom and Sparky talked about me. Maybe it's cuz it's a holiday and grown-ups are all about politeness, but they said some nice things. Sparky told Mom I'm doing well in her special after-school "history program," and Mom said she was really proud to hear that. Mom said she's thankful to have me and a nice home. Sparky said she was thankful

for every day the sun rises. I said I was
thankful for pie.

On Saturday I hung around at Sarafina's
house, and me and her and Alvaro made the
BIGGEST LEFTOVER SANDWICHES we

 possibly could.

Then we all fell asleep in
the middle of the day watching
a scary-movie marathon, and
when we woke up, Sarafina's
mom made us waffles, which we ate with ice
cream and chocolate sauce. We got real messy,
and Alvaro took a ton of pictures.

Best. Turkey holiday. Ever.

YUM!

Woof!!

Dear Diary,

OMG! ALVARO IS A <u>WEREWOLF!</u> Crazy, right? I mean, I guess no crazier than me being a Slayer, but still! He turns all wolfy on full moons. After Alvaro turned back into Alvaro, he was freaked out that <u>we</u> were gonna freak out and would call the police (or worse...animal control). The only way we could figure out how to calm him down was for Sarafina to show him some of her magic. He chilled out a lot when he realized he wasn't the only one with a secret. I didn't want to be left out of the whole corny, emotional scene, so I told him about my destiny as a Slayer, too. Sparky's not gonna like that. But it felt nice to share our secrets. We all pinkie-swore to never tell anyone else.

Even cooler? Turns out Alvaro knew all about the increase in local vampire activity. He said he could smell the vamps. We told him about our patrols, and he begged (ha-ha) to be invited. Can't wait to hear what Sparky says about this one!

Poor Alvaro got bitten by a werewolf when he was just a little kid—and he's dealt with it on his own ever since. He said it can be really dangerous for some people, usually people who have a lot of anger issues. That's why Alvaro tries to stay super-duper calm all the time.

A Slayer, a witch, and now a werewolf. That's us—my group of friends is a little gang of proud weirdos. Too bad we all failed our history project!! According to Miss Canter, "A werewolf ate my homework" is not a decent excuse!! So much for telling the truth.

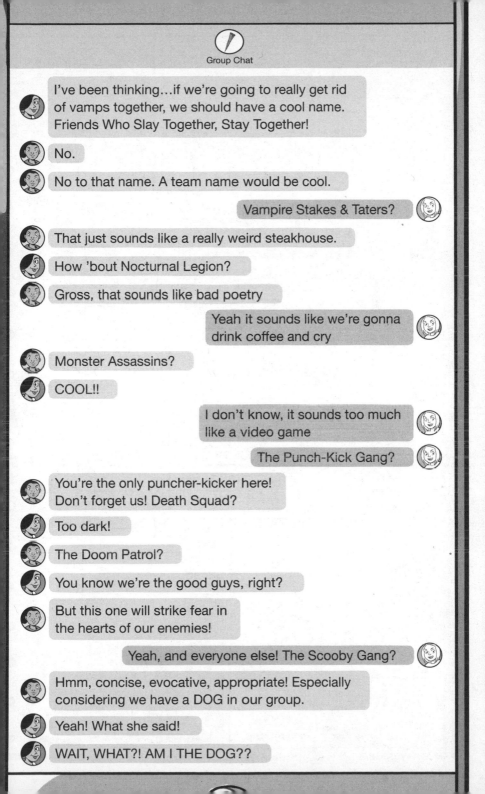

Dear Diary,

Things are going
pretty well for your old
pal Buffy. Turns out
Cleveland isn't so bad.
Date, shop, go to school,
hang out, save the world

SCOOBIES!

from unspeakable vampires—I do all that girl
stuff. Well, except dating. Boys are _gross_.

Having friends <u>helps a lot</u>—especially with
the Slayer stuff. Alvaro's second time joining
on patrol was pretty uneventful. It's silly to
wish to be attacked by vampires, but I was
kinda disappointed I didn't get to show off my
Slayer skills. Though Sarafina did manage to
save us...from starving. She used her magic to
pop a bag of popcorn. No microwave needed!

We sat around, munching popcorn, while
Sparky told us scary stories about some of
history's worst vamps:

- <u>Count DRACULA</u> is real!! (Apparently, he sold his story to become a celebrity in the human and demon worlds.)
- <u>Drusilla and Spike</u> are, like, this really popular vampire couple. She's crazy and has psychic powers, and I guess he's a poet or something?
- <u>The Primum Dominum</u> is this really old vampire who likes to settle down in a town, throw a big vampire party, and eat everyone. <u>Not cool!</u>

Okay, enough Slayer talk. As far as Normal Stuff that Normal Kids do, there's a school winter party coming up! Mom already agreed to buy me a new outfit for it, under the condition that I get at least a B— on my math test. Speaking of, I'd better go study!

Aside from tests, <u>life is good!</u>

Dear Diary,

My life is a <u>fart</u>. Wanna know why? Well, look at what Mom left taped to my bedroom door when I got home from school....

Rules for being GROUNDED

NO TV
NO phone
NO computer (except for homework)
NO video games
NO Sarafina or Alvaro
NO extracurriculars
NO desserts
<u>NO WINTER PARTY!</u>

(Parties are for kids who don't cheat on tests!)

P.S. I'll let you know when you're un-grounded. Don't ask.

Everything is officially TERRIBLE. Let me tell you something, Diary: When Joyce Summers grounds her daughter, she does <u>NOT</u> kid around.

I told Mom that Melanie is a <u>liar</u> and my <u>sworn enemy</u>, but she doesn't believe me. I'm bummed. I wish Mom would take my side, but she thinks I'm lying. She said I wanted a new outfit so badly that I cheated on my test! It didn't even occur to me to cheat! I shoulda! Then I'd be in trouble for an actual reason!

The thing is, Mom can smell lies, and since I gotta hide all the Slayer stuff from her, I must reek. She thinks I'm being suspicious—and I am—but it's not for the reasons she thinks. So I'm grounded. I have to stay in my room and have no fun, and I can't even go out on patrol cuz she's watching my every move.

On the bright side, now I can catch up on some decent sleep while I'm grounded!

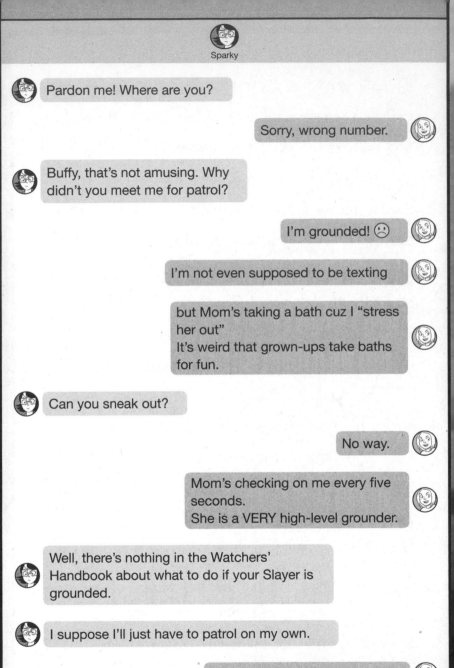

Dear Diary,

There's one thing my mom still allows while I'm grounded, and that's snail mail. I'm lucky to have two friends who will go through the effort of actually putting a stamp on an envelope and a letter in a mailbox. (Of course it takes, like, <u>DAYS</u> for it to arrive. How did people live before text messages?)

We miss u! boo hoo

I miss them <u>so much</u>!! I mean, I see them at school, but it's just not the same as talking and texting every day! I wanna <u>hear</u> the snort-laugh Alvaro does <u>only</u> when he watches bad TV. I wanna <u>see</u> Sarafina mend some small beautiful thing with her magic, like she did with my old music box. I wanna <u>smell</u> Sparky's weird books—which is just plain weird. I'm going stir-<u>CRAZY</u> being in my room 24-7!

There's just nothing more to do at home—except homework—so really it feels like all I do is go to school, come home, do homework, sleep, repeat! It's a nightmare!

I'm full of lots of Slayer energy and preteen frustration. I think I might sneak out and patrol on my own for a little bit tonight. Mom's got a cold, so she went to bed early, and I can hear her snores throughout the house. I think getting rid of vamps will help my mood. (Sparky would be so proud to hear that!)

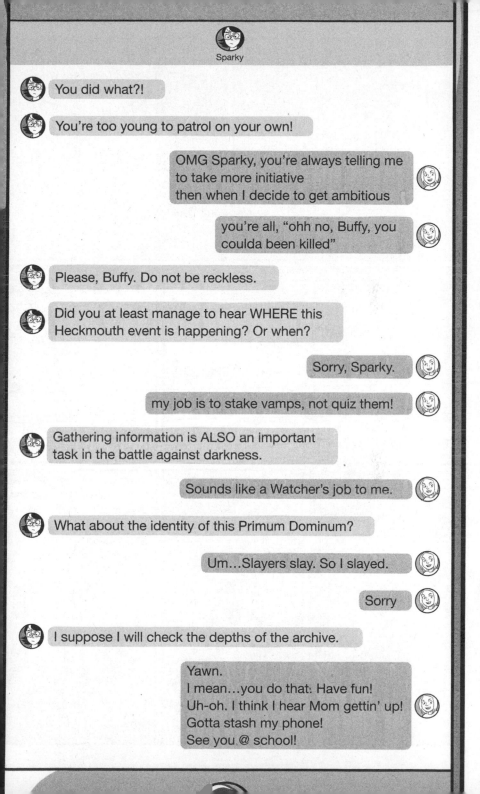

So... how was the party?

Meh
it was yawn-worthy.
On a scale of 1 to 10, it sucked.

WHAT ARE yOU tALKING aBOUT?? It was SO MUCH FUN! The music was MAJOR and there was fizzy punch and these tiny DELISH chocolate cakes—Like, SO SMALL! I HAVE NEVER SEEN A SMALLER CAKE! Oh! And they had a chocolate fountain and a hypnotist! I got hypnotized! Sarafina told me I drew a moustache on my own face!

I can't believe I missed the party of the year. I'm gonna be in therapy until I'm 30.

ALVARO!
YOUR BRAIN ISN'T CONNECTED TO YOUR MOUTH, IS IT?

What?

What did we discuss this morn?

you mean you yelling at me
cuz I said I like soggy cereal?

You deserve to be put in your place for that
but no, THE OTHER THING!

Ohhhhh, you mean when you said we should tell Buffy the party sucked so she wouldn't feel bad about missing it?

Oh. Right. I see what I did there.

Sorry Buff-ster ☹

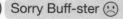

It's okay, guys.

It was fun, but not nearly as fun as it woulda been if YOU were there.

Thanks, guys 😊

Did you take any pictures?

FINA! YOU were the one who drew on my face while i was hypnotized?!

RUDE!

I missed all the fun.

Being grounded is officially the worst.

Dear Santa,

How have you been? Busy, probably! I hope things are going well up there in the ol' North Pole. You probably know this, but I've moved! My mom and I are in Cleveland now, so you'll get to our house earlier in your run! Yay! Anyways, you're probably wondering what I <u>want</u> for Christmas, so here goes:

- A scooter (to replace my broken bike!)
- New headphones! Big ones!
- Some cute sweaters—it's cold in Cleveland!
- <u>CANDY!!</u> I like chocolate. And fruity-gummy stuff, thanks. And taffy. Really, go nuts! (But no nuts, please.)
- A tablet, so I can play Jewel Swap more easily. (My Watcher got me addicted.)
- A tiny piano
- A puppy, if you're feeling <u>super</u> generous.

Good luck with everything, Mr. Claus! I'll continue to be my sweet, well-behaved self. And remember, you are <u>always</u> welcome in my house (as long as you bring gifts)!

Thanks in advance!

Buffy

Hey Diary,

Don't judge me for writing a letter to Santa.... You might think it's baby stuff, BUT I figure if vampires exist, maybe Santa does, too! Gotta keep your mind open to the possibilities...the possibilities for getting presents! Hey, I wonder if Slayers get extra presents! They totally should!

So yeah, CHRISTMAS is soon. The tree is up in the living room, and I've already made a nest of pillows and blankets right next to it so I can look at the lights every night as I fall asleep.

I am still grounded, but being stuck in the house is easier with Mom making Christmas cookies nonstop. We ate so many while we decorated the tree that I thought I was gonna barf. One more day of school left before break! I can't wait for no more homework!

Dear Diary,

It's beginning to look a lot like Christmas! Snow is weird stuff! It's going to take me a long time to get used to the whole "everything covered by a blanket of white" thing. On the plus side, the whole town looks real clean, and for some reason hot chocolate tastes a lot better.

Last Christmas, Dad and I went out in the backyard and picked little oranges from our satsuma tree and made candy with the peels. He said he'd send me fresh ones in the mail this year, but it won't be the same if I can't munch on them under the clear blue sky.

But I do love my friends. I wouldn't want to spend the holidays without them. Fina is going to have a New Year's Eve party, and Mom says I'm finally ungrounded so I can go! Which is great, cuz Mom's NYE plans are to just knit and watch British baking shows and fall asleep by nine. Santa's coming in two days! Guess we're about to find out if he's real!

Dear Diary, HAPPY NEW YEAR!

I can hardly believe the holidays are almost over. Sad-face. For Christmas, I got my Razor scooter and a bunch of sweaters, and my dad sent me the tiny piano. Mom was annoyed and said if I was gonna keep it I'd have to learn how to play it. Of course I'm gonna learn how to play it!

Fina also got a scooter, and Alvaro got a pair of Rollerblades, so we're gonna roll around together all summer. I can't wait. The SCOOBY GANG has wheels! Vamps don't stand a chance!!

New Year's Eve with my friends was so FUN! I met Sarafina's sister, Rae. They used magic to make an ice sculpture. Then we had sparkly juice and watched the Times Square ball drop. Alvaro fell asleep early, but Fina and I stayed up cuz that's what you're supposed to do at a sleepover.

Gotta go. Mom wants me to watch the finale of her British baking show with her. She said she can't handle all the tension on her own!

Buffy, I don't want to scare you but...
I think SARAFINA might be the BIG BAD!!

Alvaro, this chat is for serious business only.

 She STOLE my CUPCAKE!

It was strawberry! My favorite.
I could not resist its charms.
Also, Sparky said to look for "suspicious behavior."
I steal your desserts all the time!

Shoot, you're right.

I bet the Big Bad is Melanie.
She's definitely evil.

Yeah, but Alvaro and I have known her
since she was 5, and she's ALWAYS been evil.
But, like...normal evil. Not vampire evil.

OK but let's not rule her out.
She prob picks on me cuz she KNOWS
I'm gonna slay her someday!

 I think the Big Bad is the janitor!

Mr. Murphy? No way. He's a nice guy!
One time I threw my retainer away by accident
and he dug through the trash so I wouldn't get
in trouble with my mom!

 Awww, okay that's nice.

Being nice is kinda suspicious though.
Hmm. Who do you really think is the
Big Bad behind all the vampires coming into town?

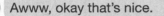

 Maybe the mayor?
I think his name is Wilkins.
I saw him talking to a snake at the zoo!
He's definitely Slytherin!

That one scary waiter at Flappyjack's.
He always forgets to put ice in my soda

I have a neighbor with, like, a hundred cats

 But cats are cool.

No, they aren't—they're evil!

You only say that cuz they don't like you.
Cuz you turn into a dog once a month.

 We've been over this!
I turn into a WOLF!!
A super-cool dark and mysterious WOLF.
NOT a dog!

My math teacher might be the Big Bad,
cuz fractions are clearly a tool for evil

MY DENTIST!
I bet he likes when I scream!

Really? I like my dentist.

 Me too.

But doesn't it make sense that a super-evil
vampire would be obsessed with teeth??

Hrmm. Maybe? Seems too obvious.

Yo Diary!

Vamps are <u>everywhere</u> lately! Me and Fina and Alvaro can barely keep up. Sparky's been goin' <u>nuts</u>, too. Each time I see her, she's got more and more paper cuts from flipping through her old books. I wonder if Slayers and Watchers get paid vacations. We sure could use one.

I've been staking a ton of old-school vampires. And when I say old-school, I mean, like <u>old</u>. This week alone I staked a vamp from ancient Egypt (I didn't even know they could <u>be that</u> old. He looked terrible.), a Roman gladiator vamp (that wasn't easy), a sad Victorian poet lady (I felt sorry for her until she tried to bite Alvaro), and—this is unbelievable, but I swear it's true, Diary—I think I dusted vampire-Abraham Lincoln. Sparky said he was just a tall guy in a top hat, but now when I look at pennies I feel guilty!!

Evil is exhausting. And worse, the vamps are getting <u>MEANER</u>. It scares me to think about.

but we almost lost Sparky to a particularly terrifying vamp. Alvaro saved the day by flashing the vamp in the face with his camera, then I staked her. She had Sparky by the neck for a half second, though, and it was the longest half second of my whole life. Sparky makes me crazy sometimes, but I really don't know what I'd do if she got hurt. It feels so weird to want to protect a grown-up, but I guess that's what I'm doing when I don't tell my mom about all this Slayer stuff. It might scare her to death to think of me running around at night, fighting bloodsuckers.

We still have no idea who the Primum Dominum is. Sparky keeps trying to reassure me, but she sounds like I do when I tell my mom "Everything's fine!"

Okay, on to happy thoughts. Tonight, I took a bath just to relax! This Slayer stuff is making me get old quick. But Mom's right.... Nothing like some bubbles to make these old bones feel new and warm.

CLEVELAND WEST MIDDLE
TOTAL SOLAR ECLIPSE
ICE CREAM SOCIAL

A rare event! Join us for ice cream on the football field as the moon passes in front of the sun and day turns to night! All students are excused from their regular classes for one hour!

Staring directly at an eclipse is extremely dangerous, so we recommend all students bring an eclipse viewer. Simple instructions for creating one out of a cardboard box will be distributed in your science class.

I can't believe I'm excited about science, but, hey! <u>No class for an hour!</u> And I can always go for <u>ice cream!</u>

You can do all the research in the world but that will never be as valuable as a vampire who's too stupid to keep a secret.

 We got very, very lucky.

Lucky?! Vamps are going to ruin the eclipse-viewing party, which means i won't get to stare at the sun and eat ice cream for an hour...

I WAS REALLY LOOKING FORWARD TO THAT!

 Such is life of a Slayer.

Sometimes keeping lots of people from being murdered means not eating ice cream.

So what do we do now? Cancel the party?

 I've already talked to the school administrators, and they refuse to budge on the matter.

 It turns out teachers want to participate as badly as the students, and you can't reschedule an eclipse.

You didn't tell them about the bad guys tryin' to suck everybody's blood?

 No, because absolutely no one would believe me.

It's strange, but the administration already sees me as something of a ZANY figure.

Yes. How strange.

What a mystery.

 Very funny.

 Barring the possibility of canceling the event, our only option moving forward is to identify and defeat the Primum Dominum himself.

Great. So we're basically exactly where we were.

 Yes. But now we have a deadline.

Grrrrreat.

 You can do this, Buffy.
I have come to trust your abilities over these last months.

I just don't know how much harder I can think about this.
I still have homework, you know!

 Slayer duties are far more important than grades, young lady.

You think so? Try telling my MOM that.

Dear Diary,

Well, we know what the Big Bad is up to now. We just don't have any idea of how we're going to stop him yet. Sparky's been buzzin' around all her big old books, trying to find some kind of super-weapon or super-Slayer move for me. Something to make sure we win against someone as old and powerful as the Primum Dominum. If only we knew who he was, we could take him out before he puts his plan into action.

I'm all full of feelings right now! I'm tired cuz hello! I'm a student _and_ the Slayer. And I'm mad, cuz I was looking forward to an afternoon with ice cream and no school! Why does the Slayer stuff always have to get in the way? I guess that sounds selfish, but I wanted to relax with my head in a box. Just for an hour. And if I'm honest, I'm scared, too. What if I can't stop this? I'm just a kid.

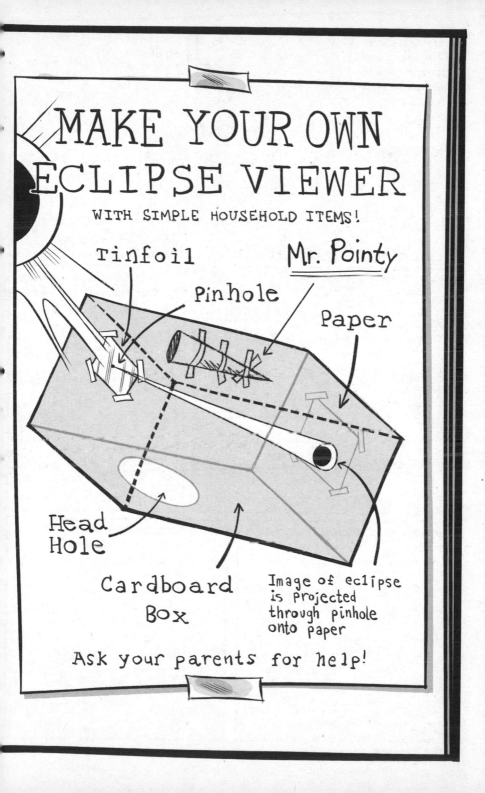

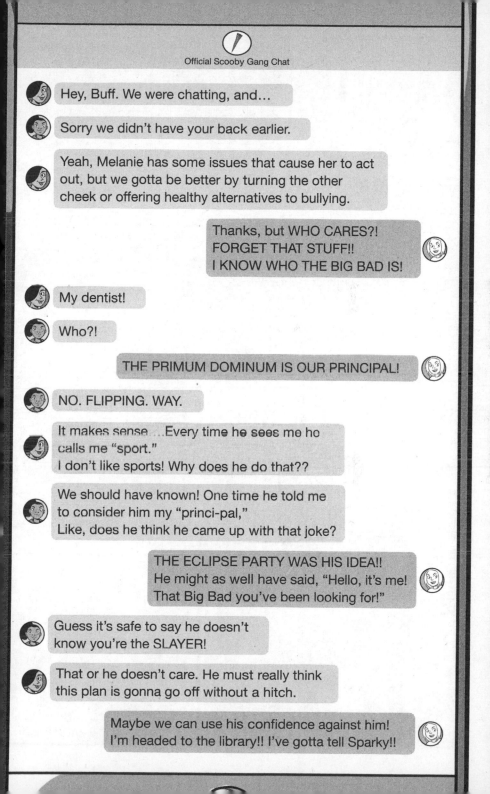

Hey Diary,

I don't even know where to start. Things are absolutely <u>CRAZY</u> around here. After I told Sparky that the Primum Dominum was Principal Masters, we ran to stake him. But when we got to his office he'd totally vanished. His secretary told us he had to go on an "emergency vacation" and would be back next week—just in time for the eclipse! Sparky's feelin' pretty dumb about not noticing her boss was a vampire. But we were all caught off guard. Principal Masters is out during the day all the time, which is so <u>not</u> a vampire thing to do. Sparky says he goes to BBQs and is on the faculty disc golf team!

I sat in the library, using my frustration to carve, like, a hundred stakes while Sparky went through her books. Turns out Principal Masters wears this thing called the <u>Gem of Amara</u>:

THE GEM OF AMARA is a mystical ring considered by many to be the "Holy Grail" for vampires. According to legend, this gem makes the wearer impervious to the usual effects of crosses, fire, wooden stakes, and other vampire-specific weaknesses. Its most uncanny effect is granting immunity to sunlight—thus allowing a vampire to hunt in broad daylight. It also strengthens the vampire, rendering him practically invulnerable!

Do you know what <u>invulnerable</u> is? (I had to look it up....) It means, "impossible to harm or damage"! That means I'm dealing with an ancient, powerful vampire who can't be hurt! Great! (In case you weren't sure, that last bit was sarcasm.)

What am I going to do? How am I supposed to defeat an invulnerable vampire when I'm just...me?

Dear Diary,

The eclipse is Friday. I'm still super worried, but Mom gave me a pep talk, and it really helped. Nice to have a mom who really <u>believes in me.</u>

Being "proactive with pep" is not enough. So tonight, the Scoobies got together to strategize and make a plan. I ended up having this kinda crazy idea, but Sparky thinks it can work. So Sarafina's puttin' some powerful spells together. Alvaro will probably turn werewolf when the eclipse happens, and he said he's ready to claw some vamps if he has to. Even Sparky wants to help out. I wish I were strong enough to do this on my own, but I'm glad I have friends who can help— even if we're all just pretending to be brave.

We hugged one other for a really long time before we all headed home. Sparky grabbed my shoulders, looked me in the eyes, and said, "Buffy Summers, we are going to be <u>just fine.</u>"

See ya later, Diary. I <u>hope.</u>

Dear Diary,

There aren't any medals or awards for being a top-notch vampire Slayer, did you know that? Sparky says, "Everyone <u>NOT</u>

CHAMPS AGAINST VAMPS!

getting eaten is its own reward," but, you know, it would be pretty neat to have a trophy or a gold-plated stake or something. And a little ceremony, where I could get up and be real classy and thank everyone who helped me defeat the Big Bad. I couldn't have done it alone.

Sparky says the faculty assumes Masters never came back from his "vacation." No one seems to care, either—I guess he was kind of a nuisance to everyone he worked with. Guess he shoulda spent less time cookin' up plots to feed kids to vampires instead of...doing whatever it is a principal does.

It feels real good to be on the other side of the Big Bad Battle. It's almost strange to think about the terrified Buffy who hadn't defeated the Primum Dominum yet. I wish I could go back and tell her it's okay to trust her friends and her mom and her Watcher. Now it feels like I shoulda known that all along. Guess that's how things like this go.

I'm going to try and remember that for next time. Though I'll probably forget. Apparently being a Slayer doesn't come with a super memory—which is why I made a C- on my vocab quiz. Grrr. Slaying vampires? Easy. Slaying vocabulary words? Not so much.

Buffy